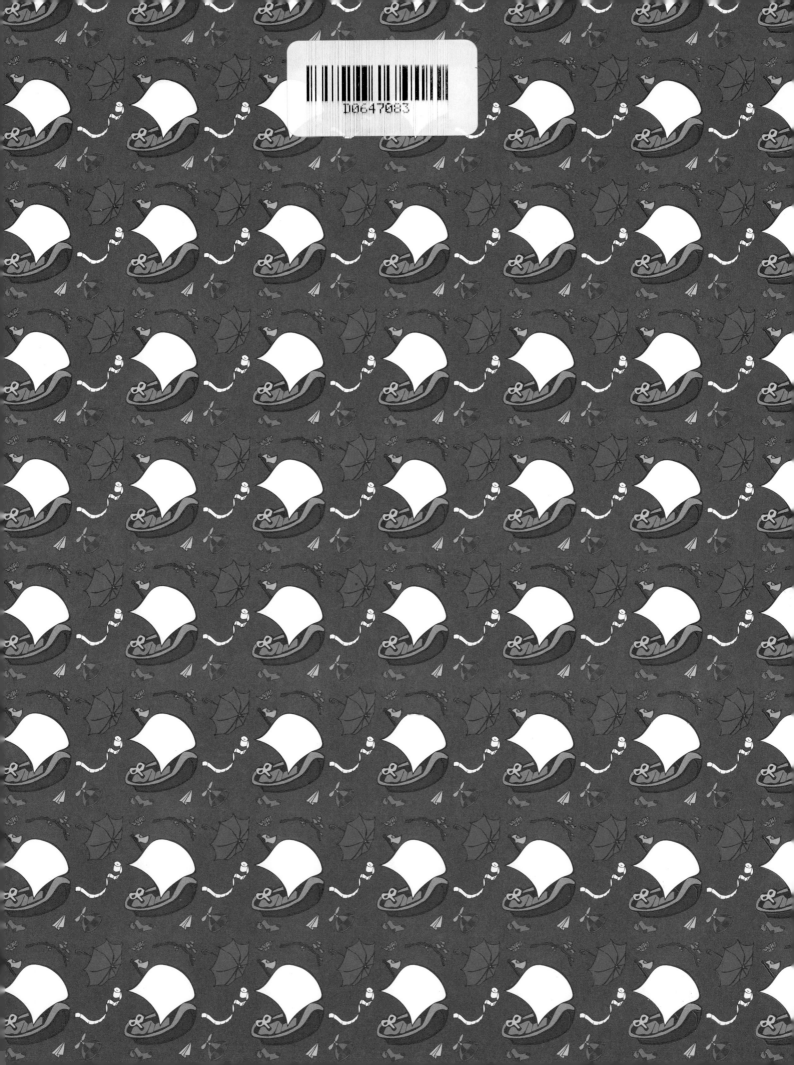

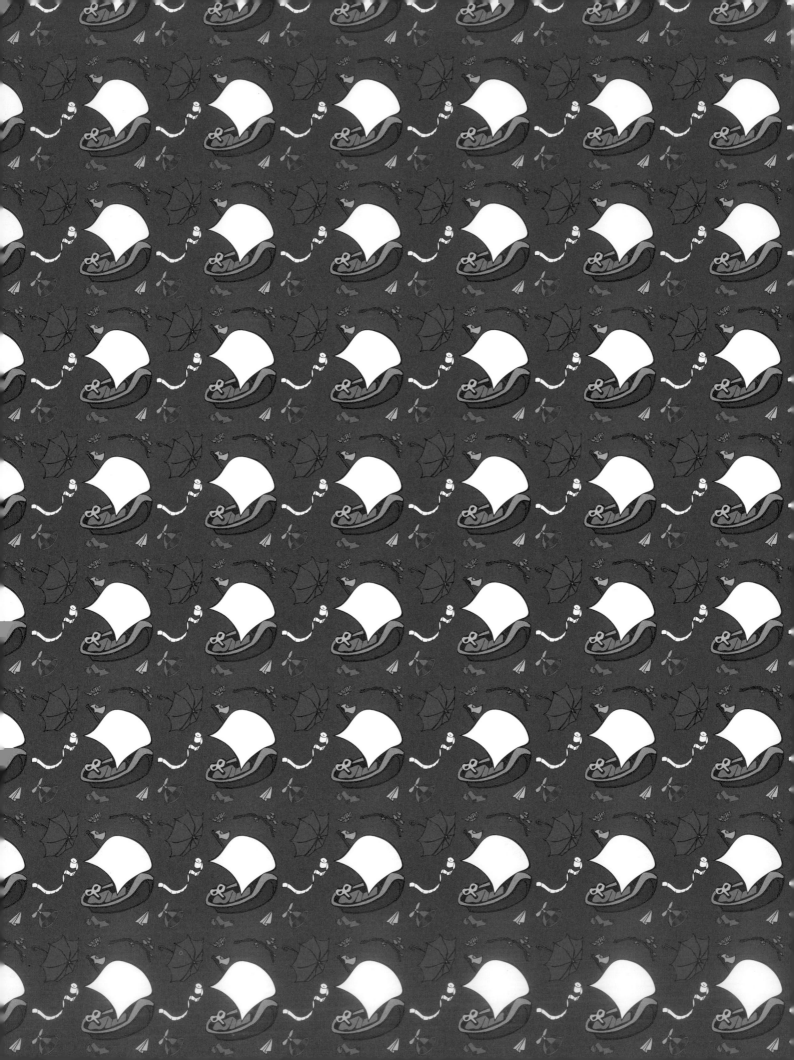

Blown Away

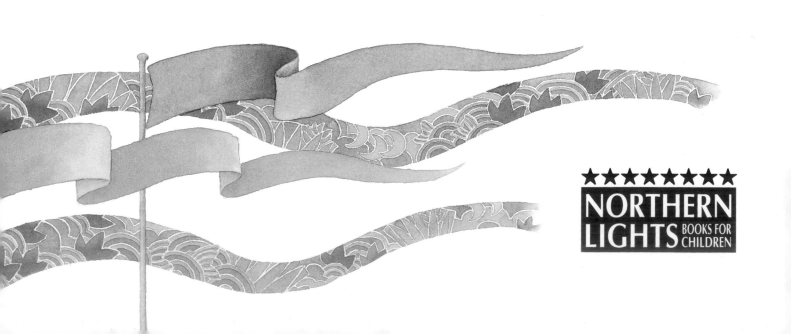

Blown Away

Story by Julie Lawson

Illustrations by Kathryn Naylor

Blown Away
Text Copyright © 1995 Julie Lawson
Illustration Copyright © 1995 Kathryn Naylor

Northern Lights Books for Children are published by
Red Deer College Press
56 Avenue & 32 Street Box 5005
Red Deer Alberta Canada T4N 5H5

Acknowledgments
Edited for the Press by Tim Wynne-Jones
Design by Kunz + Associates
Printed and bound in Canada by Friesen Printers Ltd.
for Red Deer College Press

Financial support provided by the Alberta Foundation for the Arts,
a beneficiary of the Lottery Fund of the Government of Alberta,
and by the Canada Council, the Department of Canadian Heritage,
and Red Deer College.

COMMITTED TO THE DEVELOPMENT OF CULTURE AND THE ARTS

Canadian Cataloguing in Publication Data

Lawson, Julie, 1947–
Blown away

(Northern lights books for children)
ISBN 0-88995-119-5

I. Naylor, Kathryn. II. Title. III. Series.
PS8573.A94B66 1995   jC813'.54   C95-910460-7
PZ7.L38B1 1995

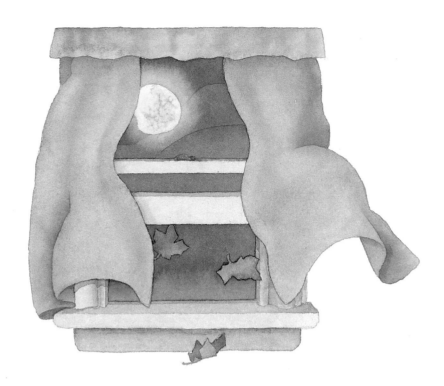

For Bob, Sue, Robyn and Tim
–Julie Lawson

For Les and Margaret
–Kathryn Naylor

On the first day of autumn

the wind picked up. It picked up leaves and
scattered them in a free-flying flurry all over the ground.
It picked up waves, whipping them into a white sea froth
across the bay. It picked up the hats and
packs of Mistaken Road children as they hurried off to school.
It picked up Molly Melinda and carried her away.

From her window on Mistaken Road,
Jess could sometimes see the giant.

And on the first night of autumn,
when she felt the wind and saw the agate moon,
she knew.

Tonight was the night.

She slipped through the open window
and raced to the maple tree where Claire and Rigby were waiting.

"Is it far, Jess? How far?"

"Way farther than far."

"Is it big, Jess? How big?"

"Way bigger than big."

"Will we get there on time?"

"Not if we keep talking," said Jess.

She flew along her secret paths,
leading Claire and Rigby across streams,
over moss-quilted logs, through tangles of old man's beard.

"Are we close, Jess? How close?"

"Way closer than close. Can you hear it?"

They stopped and listened.

"Just the wind," said Rigby.

"Only the stream," said Claire.

"Beyond that," said Jess. "Listen hard."

Then they heard it. A dry fluttering, like the unfolding of a kite.

A castle rising in the wind,
         lit by the agate moon.

                "*Is that where we go for the ride?*"

                        "*Yes!*" *said Jess.*

"Will the giant mind, do you think?"

"Oh no," she said. "The moon is right.
The wind is right. And he's in the right mood.
See? He's opened the gates for us."

They followed Jess through the gates
and up the staircase. When they reached the tower,
they leaned over the parapet, held their breath and waited.

The giant stepped onto the hilltop
and began to unreel the kite strings.

"Will it fly, Jess?"

"YES!"

The wind whistled through the strings.

Slowly, slowly — then whoosh!

Into the sky sailed the Castle of Kite.

The castle dipped and swerved and soared
and curled as the giant played the strings,
weaving his kite through the sky.
Banners streamed in snap-flapping colors.

Suddenly, the giant felt a tickle in his nose.

"A – A – A – A – CHOO!"

"Gesundheit!" said Claire.

*But the wind whisked the Castle of Kite
from the giant's hand and sent it spinning.*

"What now, Jess?"

"Where are we going?"

"I don't know.
    This has never happened before.
        I guess even giants lose their grip when they sneeze."

The wind swept the Castle of Kite

through showers of stars, far beyond the spindrift of the Milky Way.

"Maybe if we pull up the string —"

"And tie it to an anchor —"

"And drop it to the ground!"

"Who's got the anchor?" asked Rigby.

"Oh."

"Maybe when the wind dies down —"

"We'll float like a parachute —"

"Or crash," said Claire.

"Oh."

A circle of colors spun in the darkness.

"Is that a planet?"

Flecks and spatters shifted in changing patterns,
like the colored stones in a kaleidoscope.

Suddenly, the wind whirled the Castle of Kite
into the circle. But it wasn't a tumble of stones.

"There's my balloon!"

"There's my hat!"

"And there's —"

"What —"

"Is it really —"

"Yes!" they cried. "It really is Molly Melinda!"

Everything the wind had picked up was there:
    from hurricaned leaves to white sea froth, from kites and gliders to hats
    and packs, a windfall of the lost and blown away.

Claire reached out and snatched her balloon.

Righy lunged for his baseball cap.

*And Jess grabbed hold of two outstretched hands
and pulled in a windblown Molly Melinda.*

"Whew!" she said. "Am I glad to see you!"

As the Castle of Kite tumbled through the windfall,
Jess spotted an arrow aiming straight for the tower.

"Quick, Rigby!
Grab that arrow before it tears a hole in the kite!"

"Good point, Jess," he said.

His words gave her an idea.
She caught a curved branch and a passing length of twine,
then fashioned a bow. Claire wound up the kite string.
Rigby tied the string to the arrow and said,
"Who's got the sharpest eyes?"

"I do," said Jess.

She fitted the arrow to the bowstring,
pulled back, took careful aim and let the arrow fly.

They felt a sudden jerk.
    The castle quivered, then held steady.

    "Duck and cover!" said Jess
        as the windfall tumbled into the courtyard.

    Quickly, they filled their packs and pockets
        with the lost and blown away, then one by one,
        slid down the kite string.
When they reached the foot of the maple tree,
    they reeled in the Castle of Kite and left it there for the giant.

On the second day of autumn the wind was still.

"Nothing will blow away today," said Jess.
"You don't need weights in your pocket."

"You never know," said Molly Melinda.

But Jess knew.

> *From her window she caught a glimpse of the giant,*
> *striding away beyond Mistaken Road.*
> *Slung over his shoulder,*
> *carefully folded, was the Castle of Kite.*

> *"He'll fly it again," she said to herself.*
> *"One night when the mood is right and the wind is right*

and in the sky there's an agate moon."

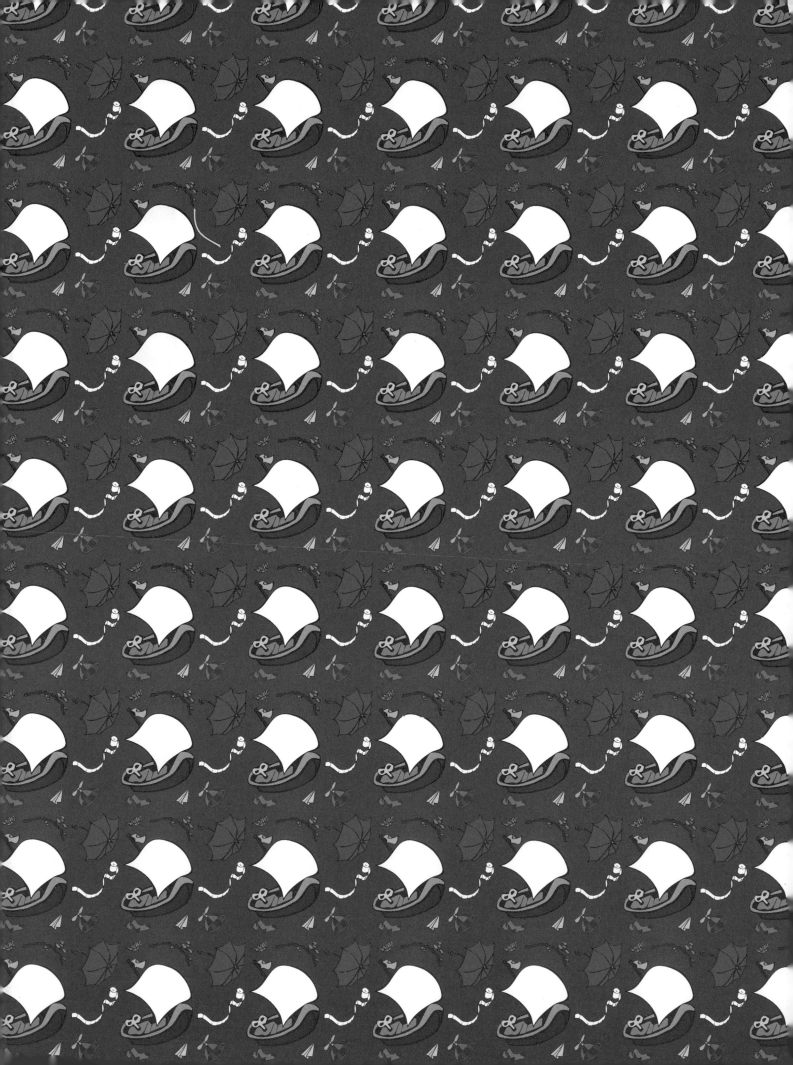

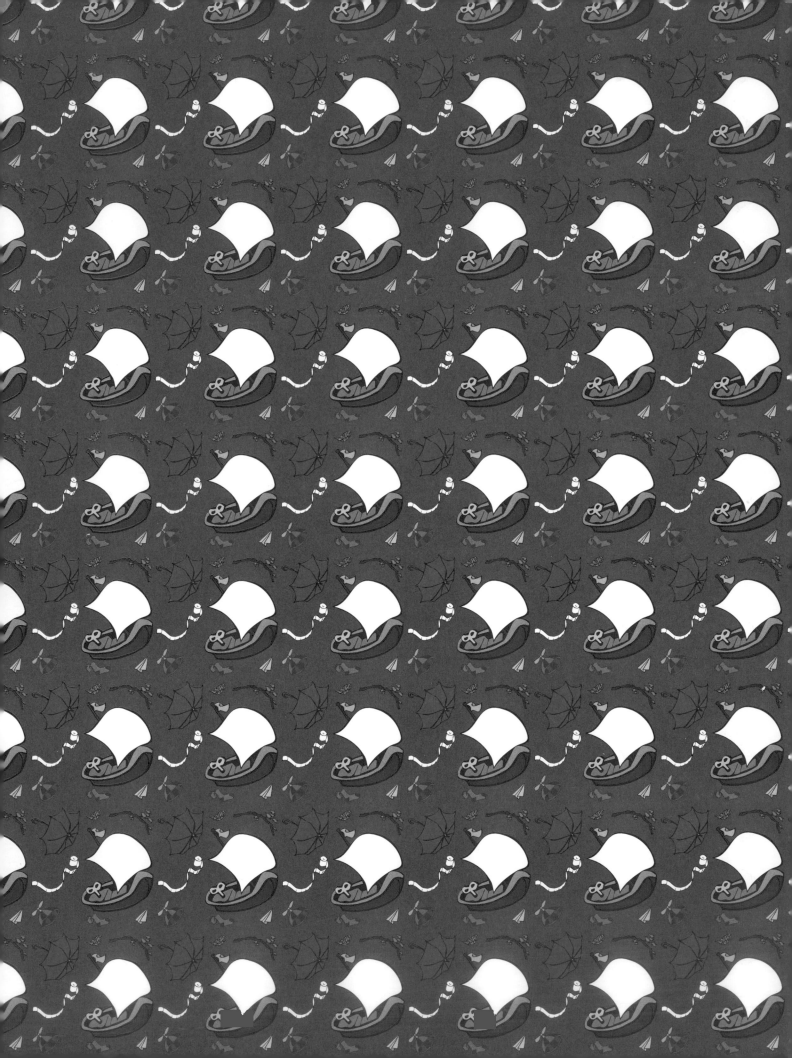